His Future Bride

A Curvy Girl Age-Gap Romance

Nichole Rose

Nichole Rose

Contents

Dedication

This one is for the self-rescuing princesses of the world. You're such badasses!

About the Book

He's not letting her get away...even if he has to keep chasing her down.

Cash

Riley Saunders is a goddess. I'm sure of it.

She's feisty and independent, and those curves of hers drive me wild.

I think I fell in love with her the second she opened her mouth and told me off.

Now I have to convince her that no matter how far she runs, I'll follow.

She's worth the chase.

One way or another, this little virgin goddess is going to be mine.

Riley

Cash Jamison is crazy. Or so I keep telling myself.

Who decides to marry someone at first sight? He did, that's who. I think he's serious.

He's gorgeous and dominant, and I might be just as crazy as he is because I want to belong to him.

But why would a billionaire who looks like him want a curvy girl like me?

He sounds like he means it when he says I'm his...but I'm so afraid he's going to break my heart.

Please chase me, Cash.

Warning

When this bossy billionaire meets his younger BBW, she's everything he didn't know was missing. Now he has to convince her that she's worth the chase in this sweet, steamy romance from Nichole Rose. If virgins, hot billionaires, and over-the-top hilarity do it for you, you're going to love Cash and Riley. All Nichole Rose books come complete with a sticky sweet and guaranteed HEA.

Chapter One

CASH

I step through the glass doors of the packed airport, headed toward the limo waiting on the curb. The sticky heat hits me like a fist, almost instantly sending my body heat ratcheting up several degrees. It feels good though, reminds me that I'm home.

My elderly driver hurries forward to grab my single bag, but I wave him off. He's been driving around for the last four hours, waiting for the tower to finally let my plane off the damn tarmac. He's probably as tired as I am.

"Welcome back to Nashville, Cash," he murmurs, holding the door open for me.

"Thanks, Lane. It's damn good to be home." I've been to London, Los Angeles, and then Miami in the last three days. I'm exhausted. I toss my bag inside the limo before climbing in after it. "We're headed to Saunders Management down on Music Row."

Lane makes a clicking sound with his tongue, letting me know what he thinks about me running straight from the airport to work. He's more like an uncle to me than anything. He's been with me since I made my first million fifteen years ago, and has no qualms about speaking his mind. It's a habit I can appreciate. I don't have time to beat around the bush and I pride myself on being a straight shooter. I say what I think and mean what I say. It's served me well thus far in life.

Hopefully, it'll serve Kasen Alexander, country music star extraordinaire, just as well today. I'm not in the talent business, but he's a real good friend and called in a favor I owe him. I guess his new manager is having problems with her Board of Directors. Something about her being too young to run a company. I'm not clear on all the details yet and I'm not sure what he thinks I can do to help, but at the very least, I owe him a meeting to hear him out.

"You can fuss at me later," I tell Lane with a small grin. "I was supposed to meet Kasen there two hours ago, but the damn pilot wouldn't let me off the plane." There was a bomb scare...which these days could mean anything from an unattended package in the terminal to an actual terrorist threat.

"A cooler of breast milk started leakin'," Lane says in his Southern drawl, shaking his gray head. "Airport security was runnin' around like the dadgum Taliban was here. The bomb squad and Feds was crawlin' all over this place."

"Breast milk? You're kidding me."

He shakes his head again.

"Jesus Christ." I throw my head back and laugh loudly. I would decide to fly in on the day breast milk shuts down the whole damn airport.

Lane's blue eyes twinkle with humor as he slams the door and makes his way around to the driver's side.

I lean back in the seat, closing my eyes. Long days and even longer nights are normal for me. When you run a multi-billion dollar company, there's always something that needs attention. I've done it so long, I've gotten used to snatching sleep wherever I can find it. Lately though, it's not been enough. Nothing is.

I feel restless and unsettled, but I can't figure out why. Nothing seems to interest me much anymore. Maybe I'm burning out. I've been burning the candle at both ends since I was twenty. At thirty-five, I'm not a spring chicken any longer. Hell, maybe that's the problem.

I'm not getting any younger and money no longer holds the same allure it once did. It doesn't keep me warm at night or fill my big house with laughter. I'm man enough to admit I'm lonely. It's been so long since I enjoyed the company of a woman, I can't even remember the last time my dick was in anything but my own hand. I need a woman.

Too damned bad I can't seem to find one that does anything for me. I'm tired of hopping from bed to bed with women who are all after the same thing: my bank account. I want something else. Someone who sees beyond the tattoos and bank account to the man beneath. I just can't seem to find her.

"How long are you home for?" Lane asks me.

"Not sure yet," I mutter, not even opening my eyes. "Doing a favor for Kasen and I need to take care of a few things. May be here a while."

Lane gives me another click of the tongue. "Good. Keep workin' like you have been and you'll be a crotchety old bachelor like me."

He's probably right.

I'm just not so sure there is another future for me, despite how fucking bad I want it.

"Kasen, it's good to see you," I greet my friend half an hour later, pounding him on the back. At six-five and two hundred and fifty pounds, I'm not a small guy. Neither is Kasen. We tower over everyone else, our wide bodies taking up more than our fair share of room in the hallway outside his manager's office.

Kasen has that all-American charm women eat up. His hazel eyes, dimple, and messy hair give him a boy-next-door vibe. With tattoos up and down my arms, unruly black hair, and icy blue eyes, I look more like a biker than a billionaire.

Even in a suit, I tend to intimidate people. Kasen, on the other hand, tends to send women swooning. Unfortunately for them, he's been hung up on the same woman since he was a teenager and can be a bit of an asshole about it. Every song he writes is about her, but he adamantly refuses to tell the world who she is. From what I understand, he left her behind to pursue music but hasn't gotten over her. It's not my business so I stay out of it.

"You too, man," he says, grinning at me. The smile doesn't reflect in his hazel eyes. It rarely ever does. "Thank you for comin'. If Riley loses the company, it's going to break her heart."

"Her Board of Directors is giving her a tough time?"

Kasen's jaw clenches. "Yeah. Her father passed away four months ago, leaving majority ownership to her. The Board thinks she's too young to run the company, so they're making her life as difficult as possible, hopin' to freeze her out."

"How old is she?"

"Twenty-one," he says, crossing his arms and leaning back against the wall. "She's damn good at her job though, Cash. The girl knows her shit. Her daddy made sure of it. She's been followin' him around, learnin' the ropes since she was a toddler."

"So she's prepared to run the company."

"Yeah, and she could do it if they'd stop gettin' in her damn way at every opportunity." His teeth grind together. "They tried to force me to accept a new manager when he died. I told them it was either her or I walked. A few others followed suit, but the Board doesn't give a shit that she's got her pick of clients."

"You trust her."

Kase nods.

I process that for a moment. Kasen is smart and has good instincts. He's also one of very few celebrities who have managed to stay out of trouble. Paparazzi love to make up stories about who he's sleeping with, but that's about the extent of the drama surrounding him. Despite the fact that he can be an asshole, especially to women trying to ensnare him, those stories never make it to the press. I'm guessing that's because of his manager, Riley Saunders.

I get what it's like trying to run a company at a young age. I made my first million at twenty and faced the same sort of opposition. Very few were willing to bet on a kid still wet behind the ears. I'm guessing the fact that Riley is female isn't helping matters any. This may be a whole new world for her generation, but for the generations that came before us, it's still a man's world and women aren't welcome.

Nothing pisses me off more than entitled men trying to keep a good woman down. My mama was single most of my life. Despite the fact she had a college degree, she made less than she was worth for years. Raises and promotions went to her male colleagues, leaving her in tears more than once.

If Kasen thinks Riley is the woman to lead her daddy's company, I owe it to him to see what I can do to help ensure she gets to do it without a bunch of crusty old men getting in her way. My mama would expect nothing less.

"Let's go see what I can do to help," I murmur to Kase.

Jesus, I hope he's right about her and she isn't completely out of her depth here. He's one of the few friends I've got. I don't relish losing his friendship by pissing him off if this chick isn't ready for the responsibility her daddy's death thrust upon her.

He shoots me a relieved grin and then pushes away from the wall. "Thanks, man. I owe you for this."

"Get my assistant and his boyfriend a pair of tickets to see your next concert, and we're square," I mutter. "He's been hounding me for weeks."

"Will do." Kasen pauses with his hand on the doorknob. "Fair warnin', Riley is... honestly kind of terrifying."

"Oh?" I cock a brow.

"She's a bossy control freak. And she's dramatic."

Great.

I grind my teeth together, knowing damn well I just got played. She better be capable of running this company or I'm kicking his ass for waiting to spring that on me at the last second. The fucker did it intentionally, waiting until I agreed to tell me I'd be working with an uptight, overdramatic, daddy's girl.

They don't tend to take it well when I tell them what's what.

Kasen flings open the door to his manager's massive office.

"Jesus fucking Christ," I whisper, staring in shock at the goddess standing beside her antique desk with her hands on her thick hips and a scowl on her ruby red lips. My heart pulses in my chest, my dick going rock hard. Her dark hair is pinned on top of her head with a pink and black handkerchief that matches her polka dot pin-up dress. She's tiny, with the sexiest body I've seen in ages. Her massive tits and thick thighs, coupled with a trim waist and that heart-shaped face are the stuff of dreams. Specifically my filthy dreams.

"I'm not bossy or dramatic, you asshole," she growls at Kasen.

"Cash, meet Riley," Kasen says, grinning ear to ear. "Riley, this is Cash."

Fuck. I think I just found my future wife.

Chapter Two

RILEY

Holy shit. Cash Jamison is hot. When Kasen said he had a friend coming to talk to me about my problem with my Board of Directors, I thought he meant some stuffy old dude in an outdated suit. Cash isn't stuffy or old or wearing a suit.

He's massive, with colorful tattoos all up and down his muscular arms. His black t-shirt clings to his body, show-ing off the muscles beneath. His dark jeans mold to his powerful thighs. There's no hiding the bulge in them as he stares at me, his blue eyes locked on my face like he just saw a ghost. Except I don't think he'd be growling at a ghost like he is right now.

The dark rumble of sound shoots straight to my core, causing my nipples to harden and my panties to grow damp. He stares at me like he's the big bad wolf and I'm dinner. I think I'm okay with playing the role of his lamb.

"*You're* Cash Jamison?" I ask, certain Kase is messing with me and this is the actor he hired to play billionaire Cash Jamison. Because billionaires don't look like this man. And Kase loves to torture me. It's pretty much his only hobby aside from pining away for Olivia, the girl he left back home.

"Yes," Cash growls. "And you're mine."

My eyes fly to his, my mouth opening into a shocked "O".

He crosses the room to me in three steps, stopping right in front of me. I tilt my head back—way, way back—to look up at him.

"Kasen didn't tell me you were a goddess," he says, his deep growl of a voice making me whimper. He shoots what I think is a baleful glare in Kase's direction. "You don't have to worry about your Board of Directors anymore, baby. I'll take care of it for you."

Whoa, Nelly.

"Excuse me?" I say, blinking at him like that's going to make him less hot and me less likely to agree to whatever he says. Because I'm not some damsel in distress and I don't care how hot he is, I'm not just going to sit back and let him make decisions for me and my company. No way.

"Your problem with the Board. Consider it solved," he says, still staring at me with those blue eyes that make my heart flutter. It's like they're stripping me bare and doing dirty, dirty things to me. I'm not sure exactly what kind of dirty things, but my hoohah seems to get the idea because she's wet and ready for him to slide on home.

I ignore my hoohah and cross my arms over my chest to scowl at him. "First of all, buddy," I say, resisting the urge to stomp my foot. "This is my company and I'll decide if you'll be taking care of anything for me. Second of all, I'm not your baby."

Cash grins at me, his eyes lighting up.

"And third," I turn to glare at Kasen, "I'm not bossy or dramatic."

"But you are a control freak," Kase says.

"There's nothing wrong with liking things to be organized and neat," I huff at him. "You're just jealous that I know more than you do about basically everything. Aren't you supposed to be writing a new album?"

"You do not know more than me. You just like to think you do."

"You're such a child."

"Am not."

"Go away."

"No."

"Fuck, you're pretty," Cash mutters, recalling my attention. He runs one thick, calloused finger across my cheek and then down the side of my throat. I fight the urge to shiver as electricity hums to life where he touched me, soaking my panties.

"Stop touching me." I smack his hand away.

"Why? I like touching you."

I ignore the way my stomach flutters over the fact that he likes touching me. "Because you can't just go around touching people even if you are a bajillionaire. I don't even know you. I'm pretty sure that's sexual harassment."

"His advances have to be unwanted for it to be sexual harassment," Kase supplies, most unhelpfully. He throws himself down on the sofa across from my desk, sprawling out like he lives here or something. He spends way too much time in my office. I need to find him something to do until he goes back on tour tomorrow so he'll go away and stop bugging me.

"Is that really a rule?" Cash asks, looking from me to Kasen.

Kase shrugs.

"Are my advances unwanted, little goddess?" Cash turns back to me, his expression somber.

Yes.

No.

Maybe?

I don't know. Ugh! He's too damn handsome. I'm used to dealing with handsome men, but this one is different. He's looking at me, touching me. No one ever looks at me like they want to eat me up. I'm thick and curvy and, okay fine, bossy and a control freak and sometimes dramatic. Men don't like that much. Except this one seems to like it a whole lot.

He's barely stopped staring at me since he walked into my office. And he smiles at me like he just won the lottery or something. It's unnerving.

"I don't know you," I mutter instead of trying to figure out if I like his advances or not.

"My name is Cash Jamison. I own Jamison International. My mom was a single mom. I have no siblings, pets, or strange fetishes. I'm allergic to shellfish. The last movie I watched was some weird horror flick about a possessed nun. I haven't dated anyone in a while. And I think you're sexy as fuck," he says and then grins like he's pleased with himself.

"You..." I gape at him for a minute and then laugh loudly. "Strange fetishes?"

"Figured we should get that out of the way sooner rather than later since I plan to be inside you as often as humanly possible, little goddess." He shrugs and then his eyes narrow on me. "Do you have any strange fetishes? Not that it matters. I'm down with whatever you're into, baby."

"Stop calling me that."

"Why?"

Because I like how sexy it sounds in that deep growl of yours.

"Because I'm not your baby."

"Not yet, but you will be soon. Have dinner with me, little goddess?"

"I'm neither little nor a goddess."

He rakes his gaze up and down my body, sending another wave of heat through me. "You look like both to me."

I need new panties. These are ruined.

"Aren't we supposed to be talking about my problem with my Board of Directors?" I ask, ignoring his invitation to dinner and basically everything else that just happened. I'm not equipped to deal with any of this. Men like him don't hit on girls like me. I'm not self-conscious about my body and I don't have low self-esteem, but I know how the world works, especially this world. I've spent my entire life in the country music business. And in this business, men who look like Cash Jamison date pretty little blondes like Carrie Underwood, not their curvy managers.

"We can talk over dinner," Cash says like that's settled.

"It's almost three in the afternoon." I skipped lunch and I'm starving, but I have a feeling spending any more time with this man than absolutely necessary is not going to go well for me.

"Then it's a really late lunch."

"Why didn't anyone come up with a word for lunch and dinner combined?" Kase muses out loud. "Sunch doesn't work and neither does Dinch."

"Lunsu sounds like a tree," Cash supplies.

"Lundin."

"I was just in London. It was raining and cold. I didn't like it. Are you ready to go, little goddess?" Cash puts his arm around me, steering me toward the door.

"I don't want to go to dinner with you and Kasen," I complain, though my feet keep propelling me forward. My body would betray me and decide to do whatever he wants it to do instead of helping me stand firm. It can't resist all those hard muscles and tattoos.

"Kase isn't invited," Cash says, shooting a very amused Kasen an apologetic look. "Sorry, man. You can be my best man in the wedding though. My woman will let you know where it's going to be."

Kase laughs loudly.

"Your woman? *Wedding*?" My voice is practically a screech, but I can't seem to modulate it.

Oh my God, I think I'm having dinner with a crazy person.

Chapter Three

CASH

"I cannot believe I let you talk me into this," Riley mutters, glaring at me from across the limo as Lane navigates late afternoon traffic, headed toward my house in Northumberland. She's got her arms crossed over her chest, which has her tits pressed up in that dress, showing off her incredible cleavage. Her leg bounces up and down like she's nervous.

Is she afraid of me?

"Come here," I murmur, reaching out a hand toward her.

"Why?" She eyes me suspiciously.

"Because you smell good and you're soft and I want you closer."

She narrows her eyes on me.

I reach out and wrap my hands around her waist, moving her where I want her. Which is in my lap. God, she smells amazing. Like vanilla and honey. She feels even better. Her soft body cradles my larger frame.

"What are you doing?" she cries, trying to get off my lap.

"Fuck." I snag her around the waist, trying to keep her still. My dick is rock hard against her plump ass and the way she's wiggling is giving him all kinds of ideas. "You keep wiggling on my cock like that and I'm going to forget I'm supposed to be a gentleman."

She immediately freezes, her breath escaping her lips in a shaky exhale. Desire flares in her gray eyes, though she tries hard to hide it by scowling at me. My girl is feisty and used to being in charge. She's also independent and intelligent. I saw the books scattered all around her office with little sticky notes peeking out like they mark her favorite passages.

She's the total package. I find that sexy as hell.

"Tell me about your company, baby," I murmur, running my hands up and down her arm because I can't stop touching her. Her skin is so damn soft it feels like silk against my fingertips. I love everything about that. I like having her cuddled up on my lap even more. She might not want to like me, but her entire body is relaxed against mine like she knows she belongs there too.

I've never been as sure about anything as I am about her being mine. I just need to give her time to get used to the idea of us...because make no mistakes about it, there is definitely going to be an us. I plan on putting my baby in her belly and my ring on her finger as soon as she'll let me.

"It's my family's company," she says after a moment. "My grandpa and his brother started it back in the fifties after grandpa left the military. When my grandpa passed, the company went to my dad."

"And then to you."

"I'm the last one left," she whispers, pain flitting through her expression. The sight of it makes my heart hurt for her. She's so young to be on her own in the world. It's obvious her family meant a great deal to her, as does their company. She's still mourning her dad, and now those bastards want her out of her company too.

"I'm so sorry you lost your dad, baby. What happened?"

"Cancer." She blinks rapidly like she's trying not to cry. "Before we even knew anything was wrong it was too late to help him. He passed quickly, and I took over."

I squeeze her arm, offering her comfort. "My mom was diagnosed with breast cancer seven years ago," I murmur. "She fought for over two years before she decided to stop treatment. She passed away not long later. I still miss her every day. Now I'm on the Board for a nonprofit that helps ensure women in underserved communities have access to free breast and cervical cancer screenings."

"That's how you met Kasen?"

I nod. "I approached him about doing a benefit when he first started making a name for himself. He jumped at the chance to help. We've been friends since. He's a good guy. So was your father. If I recall correctly, he was one of the biggest donors that night."

"That sounds like my dad," she says, smiling. "Did you know him well?"

"I'm afraid not. I only met him that once."

"He was my best friend. My mom died in an accident when I was little, so I used to follow him everywhere. He would take me into meetings and everything. I guess that's why the Board is so hesitant to trust me with the company. To them, I'm still the little girl in pigtails who played with dolls underneath the table while they talked business with my dad."

"But they're wrong about you, aren't they, baby? You're all grown up now."

She nods emphatically. "I know everything there is to know about our company. We're one of the premier management firms in the country music business. We currently represent over one hundred recording artists, including Kasen and several others who are very high profile." The note of pride in her voice makes me smile.

"Tell me about the Board."

Her smile falls. "They're stubborn and stuck in their ways. They think I'm too young and my ideas are too revolutionary. They're not bad people, just blind to the way the music world is changing. We need to be leading those changes instead of waiting until they drag us along kicking and screaming."

"What sort of changes are we talking?"

"Talent recruitment for one," she says, her eyes lighting up again. "Do you know how many incredibly talented people are utilizing social media to gain a following these days? We should be talking to these people, helping make their dreams a reality instead of waiting until someone else scoops them up to even show an interest. They already have large followings and potential. With the right management team, they could do so many incredible things."

"What else?"

"Diversity," she says. "The world is tired of seeing the same type of people singing the same songs. We need to start diversifying and adding more artists from different backgrounds and lifestyles. The world is changing whether anyone likes it or not. Country music needs to change with it by becoming a part of this new world instead of clinging to the fabric of the old. We need to include and celebrate the LGBT community, African Americans, Latinos, and anyone else with a passion for the music. Otherwise the music dies when the older generations do."

"Keep going," I encourage her, wanting to keep her talking for as long as possible. She's so damn cute when she's fired up and passionate about something. Her gray eyes are shining and her cheeks are flushed. She keeps flinging her hands around, using them to illustrate her points.

"Everyone thinks the key to saving the music is to make it sound more like pop, but that's not what people want. They can get pop anywhere. We need to cultivate more artists who will take us back to the roots of country music because that's what people want. And those artists are out there. We're just looking in the wrong places. We also need to make access to our current artists easier, give people new ways to interact with them and their music, and make it an entire experience instead of just dumping new albums into the world and hoping they catch."

"What did your dad think about your ideas?"

She clams up, shrugging. "I didn't tell him," she whispers after a moment, regret floating through her eyes. "I was still putting it all together before he got sick and then it didn't feel right to spring it all on him. I think he would have agreed with me though. He knew which way the winds were blowing and was willing to adapt to help his artists grow. It's why they loved him so much. He made sure their voices mattered and that they got to play the music the way they wanted to play it."

"How much of the company do you own?"

"A majority stake. Sixty-five percent. Why?"

"I think solving your problem might be easier than you think it is, little goddess," I murmur to her as the limo pulls through the security gates into my neighborhood. I want to solve her problem for her, tell her Board of Directors either they do it her way or they answer to me, but that's not what she wants. This company is her entire world. She needs to be the one who calls the shots. She's too independent to let anyone try to fix the problem for her...and that's not what she needs anyway. She's more than capable of handling this. She just needs someone in her corner to walk her through it.

"You're the majority owner of the company," I explain when she frowns at me. "Offer to buy out anyone who isn't willing to give your ideas a shot...or let me offer to buy them out. I think you'll find they're more willing to listen when they realize how much you're willing to put on the line for the company."

She blinks at me, her mouth gaping open. "You would do that?"

I nod.

"Why?"

"Because I believe in you," I murmur. "And I believe you're exactly the right person for the job. You're smart, you're well-informed, and you're passionate. You're also willing to fight for what you believe in and for the company."

I've taken bigger gambles on less and come out on top. This isn't a gamble though. Every instinct I have tells me she's exactly what Saunders Management needs to stay ahead of the pack. My instincts are also screaming that she's exactly what *I* need to move into the future.

"I don't know what to say to that," she whispers.

"Then don't say anything yet. Think it over while I feed you, and then you can decide. But just so we're clear, whether you agree to let me buy out more resistant members of your Board or not, I still want to help you." I grin, shooting her a wink as the limo pulls up to the house. "I also want to sleep with you, but one isn't contingent upon the other."

Chapter Four

RILEY

"You live here alone?" I ask, glancing between the mansion in front of me and the giant standing beside me. My childhood home is large, but his dwarfs it. This house could easily hold five families with room to spare. It's an absolutely gorgeous gothic mansion that looks more like someone plucked it out of the pages of a fairy tale than an actual house. Towers with legitimate parapets slash into the sky high above the steeply pitched roof and pointed arch windows. There's even a fricking moat around one side, though it's really more of a creek, but still. It looks like a moat.

"Worried I'm hiding a wife and kids from you, baby?" Cash asks, smirking at me. And good grief, that smirk! He's handsome all the time, but when he smirks, he looks delicious. Like some dark lord ready to have his wicked way with me.

"No," I say, rolling my eyes even though I was kind of worried about that. In my defense, he said he hadn't dated anyone in a while, not that he wasn't married with kids.

"I'm not hiding a wife or kids," he says, and then his brows furrow slightly. "Or an ex-wife, girlfriend, mistress, or gay lover, for that matter. I was single until approximately an hour and a half ago."

"Stop saying things like that!"

His elderly driver chuckles on his way back to the limo.

"It's true," Cash says with a shrug and then wraps a tattooed arm around my waist, leading me up the steps to the front door. He ushers me inside. "I keep telling you that you're mine, but you aren't getting it, baby. You. Are. Mine. You just have to accept it."

"What if I don't want to accept it?" I ask, slamming my hands down on my hips inside the massive foyer.

He pushes the door closed and then prowls toward me, not stopping until I'm backed up against the wall and he's pressed to me in one long, delicious line. He's so much bigger than me. His massive frame dwarfs mine, making me feel delicate and feminine. His cinnamon and fir scent swirls around me until I feel dizzy.

"I see those hard little nipples, Riley," he growls, leaning down until his face is inches from mine, his icy eyes searing into me. "I smell your sweet arousal and see the way your pulse races when I say you're mine. You want me, baby. You're just going to make me work for it." He tips my chin up. "Don't worry though, little goddess. I plan to work *real* hard to keep you satisfied."

"Cash," I say...though it comes out more like a needy whimper.

He groans loudly at the sound, crashing his mouth down on mine. His lips are soft as he consumes me alive, licking at my lips and then thrusting his tongue inside my mouth to play with mine. One hand latches around my hip, pulling me closer. The other goes to my hair, yanking out the bandana. My thick mass of hair falls, making him groan again as the dark strands slide through his fingers.

I wrap my arms around his neck, trying to fuse my body to his as his expert tongue completely ruins me for any other kiss. There's no way anyone else could ever possibly compete with this kiss. It's hot and hard, full of passion and powerful desire.

His erection presses into my stomach, making me weak in the knees.

He catches me to him, holding me still as he takes what he wants, kissing me until I can't breathe and the only thought in my head is getting naked with this man as quickly as possible. And then he pulls away with another groan.

"Fuck, baby," he says, burying his face in my hair. He's breathing hard, each rough exhale causing his chest to brush against my nipples like a soft caress. "Already know you're going to be so fucking hot for me when your pretty little cunt is finally wrapped around my cock."

Maybe now isn't the time, but... "I'm a virgin," I whisper.

"Not for long, little goddess," he says on another groan. "That little cherry is going to be mine just like the rest of you." He presses his face to my throat and kisses me gently before pulling back. "Come on and let's feed you before I show you how good it's going to be between us."

He twines our fingers together and pulls me deeper into the house. I stumble along at his side, oblivious to anything but the way my stomach turns somersaults at the thought of this man taking my virginity. I expected that to turn him off, but it didn't. I think...holy crap, I think he's serious about being into me.

I discreetly pinch myself, but judging from the way it hurts, I'm definitely awake. Which means it's probably a good thing I put on nice panties today. Because I'm pretty sure he's going to be seeing them real soon.

"You like it?" Cash asks, watching me with an indulgent smile.

I nod emphatically, trying not to moan as the warm brownie and vanilla ice cream melt in my mouth. "It's so good. I love chocolate."

"I love watching you eat it," he says, reaching down to adjust himself. He makes no secret about what he's doing. He just grabs his big dick and moves it before pushing his way between my legs, forcing me to spread them wide to accommodate him. My dress is so high up on my thighs, I'm in danger of flashing my soaked panties at him. "Give me a bite."

I scoop some up on the fork and hold it out to him. He wraps his full lips around the fork and then pulls back, his blue eyes locked on my face. I bite back a whimper, wriggling on the marble countertop where he put me after feeding me pan-seared steak and potatoes.

He's an amazing cook, which I now know is because his mom made him learn. I also know his mom taught him to cook and clean because no son of hers was going to expect his wife to do all the work around the house. His mom sounds like an amazing woman. I'm sad he lost her when it's obvious how much he adored her.

I've learned a lot about him in the last few hours. He told me all about his childhood and his company while he cooked for me. Once he finished cooking, he put me on his lap again, feeding me from both of our plates while he asked me a thousand questions about my life and Saunders Management.

He's insightful, intelligent, funny, and he says exactly what he thinks. I think I might be falling in love with him, which is completely insane because I've only known him for a handful of hours. But I can't deny the crazy chemistry between us or how I feel connected to him in a way I've never felt before. I like him...*really* like him.

"What are you thinking about so hard, little goddess?" he asks, planting his hands beside my hips and leaning toward me. He's all up in my personal space, his blue eyes locked on my face. There are little flecks of green in his eyes. The way they mix with the blue reminds me of the ocean.

"I like you."

A cocky smirk tips his lips up at the corner. His eyes crinkle in little lines. "It's not what I want, but I'll take it for now, baby."

"What..." I stop to lick my lips, drawing his attention to them. Desire flares in his eyes, turning them a stormy blue. "What do you want?"

"This." He reaches out, pressing his palm to my heart. "And this." His other hand dips between my legs, one finger sliding across the seam of my panties. He growls when he feels how wet they are, his nostrils flaring.

My stomach dips, my hips jerking as a jolt goes through me.

"I want all of you, little goddess."

"Okay," I whisper, not sure what else to say to that. Not sure exactly what he means by all of me.

"You done with your dessert yet?"

I nod.

"Good." He takes the plate from me, setting it on the island beside my hip. His eyes meet mine again, his expression ravenous. "Because I'm starving for mine. Lock your legs around my waist, baby."

For some reason, my body obeys his command before I give it permission to do so. My arms twine around his neck too, securing me to his hard body. I wiggle, fighting the urge to tell him to put me down when he slides me off the island and starts to carry me through the kitchen. My first instinct is to tell him I'm too heavy for him to carry, but he doesn't seem to even notice my weight. He carries me like it's easy.

The way he moves me where he wants me is so sexy to me. He doesn't ask for permission. He just does it. I like it more than I probably should. I trust him to take care of me. And I think I like not being in charge for once.

Even before my dad got sick, my workload was astronomical, laden with responsibility. It was up to me to make decisions for and take care of our clients. Since he died, it's all been squarely on my shoulders. I love the company and my job, but it feels good to let a little of that control go to someone else and just live in the moment for once.

"Where are we going?" I ask Cash when he carries me through the massive, well-appointed living room and then turns toward the spiral staircase.

"To our bedroom, baby."

Our bedroom?

Oh my gosh. He really is crazy.

I love it.

"I want to spread you out and take my time eating you," he murmurs, kneading my ass in his big palms. He grinds me down against the bulge in his jeans, making me whimper as my entire body reacts to the jolt of pleasure.

"I..." I swallow hard. "I've never done anything like this before."

"Good, because the thought of anyone else touching you like I'm about to pisses me off, baby. I don't share, especially not you." He stalks toward the stairs, taking them two at a time with ease. "I'm going to be your first and your last. Your only."

My stomach bottoms out, a wave of heat blasting through me. Part of me thinks I shouldn't be willing to jump into bed with him so quickly, but the rest of me doesn't care about being rational or safe or taking things slow. It's all for diving in headfirst and drowning in him. For living in the moment.

"I want to be your last too," I admit. "I think...I think I should tell you this is moving too fast, but I like it, Cash."

"Yeah?"

I nod, staring at his handsome face. "Please don't break me," I whisper, feeling more vulnerable and exposed than I ever have for anyone before. I never tell anyone because I'm supposed to be the one they lean on to get through their own grief, but I'm still struggling with having lost my dad. If Cash breaks my heart too, I'm not sure there will be any of it left to put back together.

"Oh, baby," he says, carrying me into his bedroom and then kicking the door closed behind him. "The only part of you I'm going to break is that tight little cherry."

Chapter Five

CASH

This is what I've been searching for. She's the passion that's been missing. The future I crave.

And fuck, am I starving. My entire body throbs in time to my cock, demanding I claim her before some other motherfucker tries to take her from me. She's too beautiful, too fierce and full of life. I love her. And I need her.

Now.

I yank my shirt off over my head, tossing it aside before I quickly work my jeans down my hips. A soft gasp leaves her ruby red lips, her wide gray eyes flicking up and down my body. Seeing those lips slightly parted makes me want to see them wrapped around my cock while I fuck her hot little mouth.

But not yet. Not until I get my mouth on her. The sweet scent of her arousal has been driving me crazy all evening. I want her cumming all over my face before she sucks me off. And then I'm claiming that cherry.

I stalk toward the bed, tugging her sexy pink heels from her feet. I press a kiss to the top of each foot, smiling at the sight of her little toes, the nails painted a sparkly pink. Everything about her is soft and pink. I fucking love it.I kiss my way up her body, leaving little love bites high up on her thighs. They part for me, opening wide to cradle my big body.

"Cash," she whispers, her cheeks flushing darker as I pull her dress up and then off, exposing her gorgeous body. She curves one leg inward to hide her pussy, using her hands to cover her luscious tits and soft middle.

"Nu-uh, little goddess. No hiding this beautiful body from me." I gently pry her hands away, my cock throbbing at the sight of her in nothing but sheer black lace. "You're pretty everywhere, baby. So damn soft and pink."

"Cash." Her whisper fades to a moan, her body arching toward mine as I run a hand from her shoulder all the way down to her hip. Her bra comes loose with a deft flick of my wrist against the front clasp. Her perfect tits spill out, her fat nipples sitting like cherries on top.

I lean down and capture one in my mouth.

She cries out, my name sounding like music coming from that perfect mouth. Her body writhes beneath me as I play with her tits, moving from one to another and then back again. Now that she's almost naked, her vanilla and honey scent is even stronger, making me growl and nip at her sweet skin.

I work my way slowly down her body, wanting her to feel me everywhere...wanting to get her used to sharing every gorgeous inch with me. I plan to lay claim to every single one, possess her so she never wants anyone but me, never forgets how good I can make her feel.I flick my tongue against the seam of her panties. Her taste floods my mouth. Honey, vanilla, and the sweet and spicy tang of her arousal all burst on my tongue at once. A spurt of cum shoots from my cock, my entire body pulsing with need.

"God, baby," I groan, pulling back to slide her panties down her legs. Her eyes are wide and dilated, her cheeks flushed, and her pulse racing. She's fucking perfection.

"What are you doing to me?" she asks, her voice a cute puff of sound that steals another little piece of my heart.

"Eating my dessert, little goddess." I toss her panties off the side of the bed and then spread her legs wide. A loud groan breaks from my lips at the sight of her pussy. She's bare, her juicy lips spread open to reveal her hard little clit.

"So fucking pretty," I whisper, burying my face in her.

"Cash! Oh my God!"

I growl, clamping my hands down on her thighs to keep them open for me as I eat her. She tastes like heaven, so damn good I know I'll never get enough of her cunt. I'm going to gorge myself on it every day for the rest of my life and still want more.

I lick and suck and bite, fucking her tight hole with my tongue.

She screams out as I thrust it inside her and move it back and forth before attacking her clit. Her body writhes and contorts like she's trying to get away from me. I snarl against her pussy, ruthlessly holding her in place and eating her until my face is soaked with her juices.

I damn near cum all over myself when I push two fingers inside her, trying to get her ready to take me. She's so fucking tight...I know that pussy is going to make me work hard to get inside it. I add a third finger, stretching her as I suck on her clit.

"Oh God, oh God," she chants.

"No, baby. It's Cash. That's what you scream for me. My name."

She does, her voice breaking as I curl my fingers up to stroke her g-spot while I suck on her clit. Her cunt locks down on me, gripping my fingers so hard it hurts. She flies apart for me, her cream flooding my mouth, sending my own orgasm tearing through me.

I work her through it, my eyes locked on her. I couldn't look away if I tried. She's magnificent. And she's mine.

Her body goes limp, little whimpers leaving her lips. I prowl up her body, stroking her everywhere and planting adoring kisses on her face as she comes down. Despite the fact that I just came, my dick is harder than it's ever been.

I yank my boxers off, kicking them away. There's no hiding the wet spot on them. I'm not embarrassed by it. Fuck yes, I just came all over myself watching her orgasm. It was that fucking good.

"Cash," she moans, reaching out for me with shaking hands. Her eyes are dilated and so dark they look like storm clouds. "I want you."

"I'm yours." Have been since the second I laid eyes on her. I never believed in love at first sight or soul mates or any of that shit until I saw her standing in her office with her hands on her hips and a scowl on her face. My entire fucking *world* shifted as soon as she locked eyes with me. And then she jumped Kasen's shit and mine, standing up for herself like the fierce little queen she is. I've never wanted anyone the way I wanted her when she told me who was in charge.

I'm so fucking in love with her I can't even imagine letting her go now.

She runs a hand down my chest and abs. My entire body trembles in response to her touch. My cock jerks, trying to get closer to her.

"I want in your mouth, little goddess," I murmur, coming to my knees beside her. I wrap one hand around my dick, stroking from root to tip. It does nothing to ease the ache in my balls.

"Yes, please," she moans, reaching out to touch me. "You're so big and hard. Does it hurt?"

"God, yes." Another spurt of cum spills from the tip when she touches me. My cock jerks in her soft hand.

"I don't know what I'm doing," she whispers. She sits up, her eyes locked on my dick. "Teach me."

"Stroke it, baby." My head kicks back, a groan tumbling from my lips when she wraps her hand around me, brushing her thumb over the tip. "Yeah, just like that. God, that feels good."

Her eyes light up at my praise, her hesitant grip firming as her confidence grows. She glides her hand up and down my length a few times, exploring. Her tongue peeks out from between those perfect lips, flicking against the head.

I groan loudly and then cry out her name when she sucks me into her hot little mouth and moans. It takes every ounce of willpower I have to keep from cumming as she sucks me, her lips stretched wide around my girth.

She grows bolder, taking more. Her eyes roll back in her head. Her tongue runs across my cock. Another moan tumbles from her lips, vibrating against my dick.

I break.

"No more," I gasp, pulling away. I need to be inside her or I'm going to lose my damn mind. "Lay back, baby. I want that cherry now."

She does as instructed, settling back on the bed as I move between her legs and hitch one smooth thigh over my hip. She's so wet her lips glisten with her juices.

"I'm not wearing a condom. I'm breaking that cherry with my cock bare, little goddess." I slide my cock through her sticky folds, coating myself in her cream. It feels so good. There's no way I'm going to last long. "Gonna plant my baby in you too."

"Cash." She melts beneath me, her eyes blazing with desire and her legs opening wider, inviting me in. "I need you."

"You have me." I take her mouth in a hard kiss, trying like hell not to cum too soon as I push my way inside her. She's so damn tight, so fucking hot. Her tight cunt resists me for a long moment before the head of my cock finally slips inside.

Her nails dig into the tattoos on my shoulder blades, a pained whimper coming from her lips.

"Shh, baby, shh," I soothe, kissing her over and over. I hate causing her pain, but it'll be over soon. "You're doing so good. Just hang in there, little goddess. I promise I'm going to make it better for you."

I stay still until she relaxes underneath me and then grit my teeth and rock my hips forward, sheathing myself in her in one quick thrust. Her cherry pops against my cock. I fight the urge to roar as satisfaction rips through me. She's mine now.

She cries out in pain, clawing at my back.

"You're doing so good," I murmur to her.

"Cash." A tear courses down her cheek, wrecking me.

"Kiss me, Riley."

She offers her mouth up to me like an eager little sacrifice, desperate for a distraction from the pain. I nip at her bottom lip before sliding my tongue against hers in a fierce kiss. I don't stop until she's wriggling beneath me, her body relaxed once again.

I break the kiss, sliding almost all the way out of her cunt at the same time and then gliding back in with a slow thrust of my hips.

"Oh," she whispers like she's surprised there's no more pain.

"You okay, baby?" I check just to make sure. As desperate as I am to move, I won't do it until I'm sure she's feeling nothing but pleasure.

"Yes. More, please."

"Gladly."

I fuck her slow, rocking into her in gentle pulses to get her used to me. She cries out my name, locking her legs around my waist and whimpering the word *more*. She's so fucking sexy begging for my cock. I can't tell her no. Don't want to.

I plant my hands on the bed on either side of her head and thrust harder. "Goddamn, you feel good," I growl.

"So do you. So good, Cash."

Fuck. Her little whimpers break me all over again. My control snaps, leaving behind nothing but the desperate need to move, to *fuck* until neither of us can take any more.

I fuck her hard, pounding into her until my balls slap against her ass with every powerful thrust.

She cries out, clawing my back and writhing beneath me.

"You gotta cum for me, baby. Need to feel you creaming all over my cock before I fill your cunt with my seed."

"Yes, yes," she chants, delirious with pleasure. "Feels so good. Please don't stop. Please don't stop."

My balls draw up, pleasure blasting through me as she begs for more. I push her leg up toward her chest, changing the angle so my cock slides against her g-spot on every hard thrust.

She screams my name, her perfect little cunt locking down on me as she creams all over me. The tight grip of her pussy rips my orgasm from me, stealing any semblance of control. I roar her name, fucking her so hard the bed rattles beneath us. Cum pumps from my cock so hard it hurts.

I give it all to her, not stopping until I know she's going to feel me dripping down the insides of those thick thighs for days. She's going to feel me everywhere, every time she moves. And she's going to know she's mine, that I claimed her.

When the waves finally recede, the last drop spilling into her, I collapse beside her, pulling her into my arms. She cuddles up against me with a soft sigh that makes my heart pulse with emotion. Fuck, I never knew it could be this damn good. I'm keeping her, no matter what anyone says.

"Never letting you go, little goddess," I mumble to her in warning, pressing a kiss to her sweaty crown. "You belong to me now."

"'Kay," she whispers back.

Chapter Six

RILEY

The sun hasn't even risen when I wake up because Cash's big body is like a furnace where he's practically lying on top of me. He took me twice more before we both passed out from exhaustion. My entire body is sore in the best way possible. I revel in the way it feels to be in his arms. He holds me like I'm precious, something he wants to protect. Even in his sleep, he cradles me carefully.

But I don't know how to do the whole morning after thing. He said a lot of things yesterday that I really want him to mean. In the heat of the moment, I'm sure he did mean them.

But will he still feel the same in the light of day?

The longer I lay here, the more the thought of him not meaning any of it stresses me out. I want what I had a taste of with him yesterday and last night. I want to belong to him. And it's going to break my heart if this was just a one-night thing for him or something he does often. To me, what we shared meant everything.

I thought I was falling in love with him yesterday, but somewhere over the course of the night, I became certain of it. I'm so ridiculously in love with him. I don't know how it happened so fast, but it did. And I would much rather live with not ever knowing if he feels the same way than with having my heart broken if he wakes up and hustles me out like last night didn't mean everything to him too.

Panic claws through me at the thought of him sitting me down to tell me *it was great, but....* I've seen too many of my clients have that same conversation the morning after. Watched too many girls leave hotel rooms in tears when some handsome man who said all the right things in the heat of the moment then dashed their dreams of happily-ever-after into little pieces.

I slowly inch my way out from underneath Cash, moving carefully so I don't wake him. I hold my breath the entire time, praying he doesn't wake up.

Thankfully, he doesn't.

But I don't breathe easy until I've gathered my clothes in the murky pre-dawn light and slipped out into the hall to don them. All the lights are still on in the house, illuminating his marks all over my body. The sight of them sends waves of heat and sadness through me simultaneously—heat because I remember exactly what it feels like to have him all over me, sadness because I know they'll fade soon.

Once I'm dressed, I tiptoe down the stairs. I was too wrapped up in Cash to notice much last night, but his house is incredible. The floors are gorgeous hardwood, with gleaming wood tables and dark furniture. The paintings hanging on the walls are beautiful landscapes that look so real I want to step into them and marvel that there are places in the world that actually look like this.

Instead, I search around for my purse, only to realize I didn't bring it. I was so wrapped up in him, I didn't even think about the fact that my purse and phone are still sitting on my desk in my office. My assistant and close friend, Cami Porter, is probably freaking out right now. I never leave my phone.

I briefly consider leaving Cash a note, but when I can't figure out what I'd even say to him, I strike the idea. Tears pool in my eyes at the thought of this being over between us before it even started, but I won't be one of those sad girls who sleeps with someone stratospheres out of their league and then turn one night into some big fairytale romance in their minds. I have more self-respect than that...or so I tell myself.

I slide my heels onto my feet, brush my fingers through my dark hair in an attempt to tame it into some semblance of order, and then slip out the front door in search of the guard shack. I wasn't paying a whole lot of attention on the way here, but I know we're in Northumberland. I've been here a thousand times before to visit clients who live in the exclusive, gated community.

Walking the half mile to the guard shack in heels is more work than I anticipated. By the time I make it there, I'm sweating and out of breath. I probably look a hot mess too. Mustering up my courage, I rap sharply on the window to get the attention of the guard dozing inside the booth.

He jerks upright in his chair, blinking at me like an owl. He's maybe twenty, with big ears and a cowlick. Once he realizes I'm not a figment of his imagination, he hurries outside to greet me. His eyes linger on what I can only imagine is my wild sex hair before doing a discreet sweep down the rest of my body. His eyes widen before he quickly schools his expression. I'm guessing I'm probably not the first walk of shame he's seen since coming to work here.

"Can I help you, Miss?" he asks, his tone polite.

I fake a bright smile. "I'd like to use your phone to call a cab, please. I seem to have misplaced mine."

"Oh. Of course." He fumbles in his pocket. "I have the number for a taxi saved."

Yep. I'm definitely not his first walk of shame.

I briefly wonder how many former participants in said walk came from Cash's house and then decide I don't want to know if I'm simply one of many. My heart rebels at the thought, telling me that isn't Cash. That he's not a manwhore and what we shared last night meant as much to him as it did to me...but what does my heart know?

Cash, my subconscious whispers to me. *It knows Cash.*

God, I miss him already. I miss the way he touches me and kisses me, and the way his deep voice washes over me, making me feel still and peaceful when I've never been very good at either. I'm always on the move, always trying to be everywhere and do everything. I don't like to sit still and let other people make decisions. I always want to be right there in the middle of everything, controlling the situation and taking care of everyone. I've been that way for as long as I can remember. I'm a bossy control freak, exactly like Kasen said.

Except for last night. With Cash, I didn't have to be in charge of everything. He guided me, taking control. He let me explore, but he was in charge and we both knew it. We both loved it. For once, someone else was taking care of me instead of me taking care of them. Not because he didn't think I could do it by myself, but because that's who he is too.

Maybe my heart does know him.

But I've never felt like this about anyone before. I'm so afraid he doesn't feel the same way.

"Your taxi will be here soon, Miss," the guard says.

"Thank you," I whisper, blinking back tears.

"Where have you been?" Cami practically shouts at me when I stumble off the elevator to my office two hours later. She jumps up from her desk and rushes toward me, her long skirt swishing around her legs. Her green eyes are wide and full of worry. "I've been calling you since I got back from the doctor yesterday afternoon. Kasen told me you were taking the rest of the day off, but I thought he was joking. You never take time off."

"I forgot my phone," I mutter, taking a gulp of my coffee as I rush toward my office as fast as I can in my heels. "It's still in my desk."

Cami stops walking, her mouth popping open. "*You* forgot your phone?"

"It's a long story." I stop outside my office door and groan loudly. "I need your key. Mine is in my purse, which is also still in my desk."

Cami eyes me sideways and then hurries back to her desk to grab her key to my office. Once the door is unlocked, she follows me inside, staring at me like I've lost my mind. Maybe I have. I don't know. Everything is still all jumbled up. And I miss Cash.

Maybe it's my imagination, but I still smell him in my office. Or maybe I still smell him all over me. I don't know. I went home long enough to hop in the shower and change clothes before rushing here to deal with everything that didn't get done yesterday afternoon. I'm desperately trying not to obsess over him, but that's all I've done all morning.

"Have you confirmed Kasen's hotel in Atlanta?" I ask.

"Yes," Cami says. "The suite will be ready when he gets into town. I've also confirmed that everything he needs for the concert has arrived at the Tabernacle and is ready to go. I also scheduled Randy for the morning talk show circuit, have the details confirmed for Luke's birthday party, and someone at ABC wants to talk to you about getting Kasen on *Dancing with the Stars*."

I glance up at her. "You're kidding me."

"Nope." She shakes her head and then giggles. "I told them he'd say no, but they want to hear it from you. I'm just a lowly assistant."

"You should be a star," I mutter. We've had the same conversation at least a million times. She doesn't want to be a musician though. She has the voice of an angel, but she's incredibly shy. Like me, she's thick and curvy. She's beautiful, but she got bullied about her weight a lot growing up. It made her hesitant to put herself out there.

"But you're right about Kasen saying no," I say when she shoots me a deer-in-the-headlights look and rapidly shakes her head. "It'd be great for publicity, but he's not going to do it. Besides, he's in the middle of a world tour."

"And he hates dancing. And television." Cami's brows crinkle. "Actually, I think he hates everything except music and you. He's always nice to me, but he's kind of an asshole to everyone else."

"That's just Kasen." He's been that way for as long as I've known him. Women throw themselves at him, but he shuts them all down. And he's not nice about it. He's still in love with Olivia Scott, his girlfriend back home. But that's not my story to tell, so I keep my mouth shut and keep his secrets. He drives me crazy most of the time, but he's my friend as well as my client. He lived with me and my dad for a while before he made it big. He's honestly like a brother to me.

"I emailed you the contact information for the rep at *Dancing with the Stars*. I also suggested Logan Hayes as an alternative to Kasen."

"I'll touch base with them today," I promise, plopping down at my desk to fish my phone out of my purse. I expect to find at least a dozen missed calls and texts from frantic clients, but the only text is from Kasen. Cami really is an incredible assistant, more than capable of handling things if I take a day off.

I open the text from Kasen.

Kasen: It's mildly concerning that your pin cushion/voodoo doll looks like me. Be nice to Cash. He's a good guy and for some reason, he seems into you. Call me if you need help dealing with the Board. I'll see you in Miami next week. By the way, you need a new pin cushion. Something happened to yours.

I glance at my desk to see my pin cushion, which only mildly looked like Kasen's annoying face, is missing. The jerk probably stole it. I read his text message again, specifically the parts about Cash. Guilt and regret whisper through me.

"I think I messed up," I mumble to Cami and then drop my head to my desk, groaning.

"You never mess up."

"I did this time." The longer I'm away from Cash, the more certain I am that sneaking out of his bed at dawn was a bad move. I freaked out, plain and simple.

"What happened?" Cami asks, her voice soft.

"I met someone," I whisper, lifting my head to look at her. She's propped up against my bookcase, watching me carefully. "I really like him."

"You like him?"

"I spent the night with him."

Her eyes widen. She knows how significant that is for me. I'm not the only virgin in the building. Well, ex-virgin now. Whatever. Cami's never slept with anyone either, so it's not like I was a unicorn or whatever.

I exhale a sharp breath. "And then I snuck out this morning."

"You didn't."

"I did," I groan, hiding my face in my hands. "He's incredible. He's so hot and kind of bossy, but in a sweet way. He offered to buy out the Board members who won't agree to give my ideas a shot."

"Wow," she whispers.

"Right?"

"So why did you leave?"

"Because I'm an idiot!" I cry, throwing my hands out. "I'm pretty sure I'm in love with him and I'm freaking out because I'm scared he doesn't feel the same way. I mean, it feels like I've known him forever, but we've known each other for less than twenty-four hours. What if he gets to know me and decides we should have left it at just one night?"

"I guess that could happen," Cami says, her expression thoughtful. "But what if you're wrong and he wants more than one night, Riley? You're the one always telling me to live a little. Maybe you need to take your own advice."

"He's not like I am," I whisper, averting my gaze. "He's really, really hot. Like his body is perfect. He literally has an eight-pack, and a massive...never mind. He's a billionaire. He could have anyone he wants. Why would he want me?"

"Because he's in love with you."

I gasp, flying up out of my chair at the sound of his voice. He's standing at the door, his arms crossed over his massive chest, his handsome face set in a hard glare. He's dressed in another tight t-shirt and faded jeans, his tattoos on full display. His hair is wild, like he didn't bother to tame it before coming here. He honestly looks like he tossed on clothes and came straight here. He's still sexy as hell.

"Cash," I whisper, my heart leaping toward my throat. "You're here. Why are you here?"

"Because you're here," he growls, stomping toward me with a hungry look in his eyes. "You're in so much trouble, little goddess."

I gulp.

Chapter Seven

CASH

I stalk across Riley's office toward her, not sure if I want to spank her ass or kiss her breathless. I wasn't surprised to wake up without her in my bed. I knew she was going to make me work to keep her. She's independent and fierce, with a spirit to match. I'm perfectly fine with chasing her pretty little ass down for as long as it takes to make her realize I'm not going anywhere without her. She's worth the chase.

I am *not* fine with her thinking she's somehow less than I am.

Maybe it was wrong of me, but I eavesdropped on her conversation with her friend. I heard her admit that she's in love with me—which is a relief since I'm in love with her too. But I also heard the worry in her voice when she asked why I would want her.

How could anyone not want her?

She's a goddess. One I want to worship for the rest of my life and whatever comes after.

I drag her into my arms, crashing my mouth down on hers. She resists me for a split second before she whimpers into my mouth and then melts against me. I lift her up, planting her round ass on her desk. Her neatly ordered supplies fall off the other side with a clatter. I ignore it. I ignore the soft laugh of her friend too, completely focused on my woman.

Her body trembles as she wraps her arms around my neck, clinging like she never wants to let me go. I flick my tongue against the seam of her lips until she opens, letting me get a taste of that sweet little mouth of hers.

Once her taste hits my system, soothing the worst of my frustration, I back off, placing little kisses at both corners of her mouth and then her forehead. My dick is rock hard. I ignore it for the moment, tucking my woman's face into my chest. A sense of peace settles over me, allowing me to breathe easy for the first time since I woke up to find her gone.

The door to Riley's office closes with a soft snick, alerting me to the fact that her friend stepped out to give us a little privacy.

"I panicked," Riley whispers, her voice small. She lifts her head to look at me, guilt burning in those gray eyes. "I've never done any of this before and you probably have and it freaked me out that maybe I was reading too much into things. I don't want to be one of those girls who sleeps with someone once and then starts planning an entire future and that's what I was doing and—"

I kiss her again, silencing her rambling explanation.

Once she melts into me again and her eyes are sufficiently dilated with pleasure, I plant my hands on either side of her hips, putting us at eye level. "First of all, I love you. We'll talk later about the fact that I had to hear you tell your friend that before you told me." I bite back a chuckle when she gulps, her eyes widening. "Second, I meant every damn word I said when we were together, Riley."

"I–"

I hold a hand up, halting her. "Third, I'm not mad you weren't in my bed when I woke up this morning. You're independent as hell and you're used to being in control. I knew giving it up to me last night would spook you, little goddess."

"You did?" She gapes at me.

"Yeah, I did. You've never had someone take care of you before me. Had you not worn me out, I would have had a car waiting to take you home. I'm not thrilled about you hiking down to the gate in those heels of yours in the dark."

"It wasn't very much fun," she mutters. "And I had crazy sex hair."

I smile at the hint of annoyance in her voice over the fact that I fucked up her hair. She's going to have to get used to it because I plan on messing it up frequently.

"Why am I in trouble if you aren't mad about me sneaking out of your bed?"

"I'm pissed you think you're less than me, baby." I tilt her chin up until our eyes connect. "You're beautiful, Riley. You've got the sexiest curves I've ever seen in my life. I love how soft you are and how perfectly we fit together. I also love those tits of yours and those thick thighs and round ass. I love how your eyes light up when you're talking about something you love, and how everything you feel shows on your face. I love that your lower lip is plumper than your top lip, and I love the little freckle behind your right ear."

"I have a freckle behind my ear?" she whispers, reaching up like she expects to be able to feel it there.

"I love how pink your cunt is and how tight you grip me when you're cumming all over me. I love the way you scratch and claw like a little kitten when I'm inside you, and the way you beg and whimper." I pull her hand away from her face when she covers it like she's embarrassed. "I also love how passionate and intelligent you are. And how you care about the people in your life and how sweet you are. Even though your Board is fighting you, you still made a point to tell me that they're good people."

"They are good people."

I smile at her again, running my thumb along her knuckles. "There is *nothing* about you that is less than me, little goddess. Anyone can have an eight-pack and a big dick, or a small waist and a big bank account. Not everyone can see the good in people who have hurt them. And there is no one else out there who makes my entire fucking body light up like the 4th of July the way it does simply by being near you. You're so much more than you realize."

She stares at me for a long, silent moment. Her gray eyes are watery, her expression soft. "I can't believe you noticed all that about me."

"I haven't stopped noticing you since I saw you standing not two feet from here, ready to give Kasen hell for calling you bossy and dramatic," I say, grinning at her.

"I am bossy and dramatic. And a control freak."

"That's all right with me, baby." I sit down in her chair, pulling her off her desk and into my lap. "I know you're only bossy because you want the best for people and you're doing your best to make that happen. You love hard and you fight hard. What you call dramatic, I call passionate. And I think it's fucking hot that you're willing to take charge and get shit done." I tuck her against my chest, loving the way she snuggles into me with a content little sigh. "You don't have to do it all on your own any longer though, baby. It's my job to take care of you so you can take care of everyone else."

"I liked you being in control last night," she murmurs. "It felt good."

"Yeah?"

She nods.

"You done freaking out now?"

"I think so." She sits silently for a moment and then tips her head back so she's looking at me. Her gray eyes run across my face, a little crease between her brows. "I've never been in love before. I might mess up again."

"I've never been in love before either," I say, smiling at her. "I might mess up too. We'll figure it out together. I plan to spend the rest of my life with you, so we've got plenty of time to get it right. But you gotta talk to me when you get freaked out. I don't like you getting all worked up and running off."

"Okay," she whispers.

"I love you, little goddess."

"I love you too, Cash."

My heart pulses, happiness washing through me in a warm flood. I tip her face toward mine and kiss her, nibbling on her lips until my dick throbs, demanding attention. He's not getting it though. Not right now. I know she's probably sore after last night and needs a little recovery time.

"What do you want to do now?" I ask her, reluctantly breaking the kiss.

"I really want to pick up all the stuff you knocked off my desk," she mutters. "It's going to take forever to fix it all."

"I'd say I'm sorry, but it'd be a lie."

She narrows her eyes on me and then her expression softens and she shakes her head, smiling. "You're going to be a pain in my ass just like Kasen is, aren't you?"

"Definitely." I grin at her. "But I'll make it good for you, baby. Every time I piss you off, you just take a seat on this cock and I'll make it all better."

"Cash! You can't just say things like that in my office."

"Why not? It's true." I consider telling her that I'm going to be fucking her in this office real soon, but decide to keep that one to myself. I just got her calmed down. I don't need her getting all riled up again already. Especially when I can't even enjoy it until her tight little cunt recovers from last night.

"Someone might hear you."

"They're all going to know you belong to me soon enough, little goddess. As soon as my baby starts growing in that belly, there won't be any hiding it." Just as soon as she'll let me, I plan on putting a ring on her finger and giving her my last name too. I want everyone to know she's mine.

Her hand goes to her stomach and I know she wants the same thing. I'll give it to her. She'll be taking my cock day and night until she's pregnant.

I slide her off my lap onto her feet before I manage to forget she's sore and spread her out across her desk. "You better pick your shit up, baby. We've got things to do."

"What things?"

"Your Board," I tell her, sliding the chair back so I can stand too. "I'll let you handle them because this is your company and you're a bad-ass, but I want them to know today that they're not going to be stressing you out anymore."

Chapter Eight

RILEY

"Kasen, will you shut up and stop bugging me?" I growl into the phone, contemplating hanging up on him. He's been annoying me since his plane touched down in Atlanta.

"Not until you promise that Cash is alive and well," he says.

"Cash is more than fine," Cash drawls, strolling into my office.

My entire body starts humming as he prowls toward me, Chinese takeout bags in hand. He's been here all day, learning about the company and what I do. He's even offered a few suggestions of his own to help with diversifying and finding new ways to help support and promote our artists. He's really smart and catches on quickly. It's not hard to see why he's such a good businessman.

With him by my side, dealing with my Board of Directors was a lot less frustrating than usual. They're all old and stuck in their ways, but they all know who Cash is. They eyed him with various degrees of respect and awe as he loomed at the end of the conference room table, letting me handle business. I know he was eager to jump in and handle the situation for me, but he didn't. He just hovered and scowled and let me have my say.

I won't say they were thrilled to hear what I had to say, but they all listened. We may end up having to buy out a couple of them, but I think the rest are willing to give me a chance to prove that I'm right. I think knowing Cash believes in me enough to buy out everyone who doesn't made them all a little more receptive. I mean, the man is a freaking billionaire with one of the most successful companies in the world. They would have been crazy not to have faith in me when he does.

It also probably didn't hurt that, before we left them to think through their options, he slammed one big hand down on the table and told them all if they thought they were going to drive me out of my dad's company, they were going to have to go through him and every single one of our clients to do it. I probably shouldn't be happy that he basically threatened a bunch of old men on my behalf, but it made me love him even more.

As soon as he reaches my side, he sets the takeout bags down on the desk and pulls me out of my chair. His lips meet mine, hot and hungry. He kisses me like he hasn't seen me all day, even though he only left twenty minutes ago to get us dinner.

"Fuck, you taste good," he mumbles, picking me up. My legs go around his waist. His fingers dig into my ass, grinding me against the bulge in his jeans.

I moan loudly.

"No!" Kase shouts. "You are not allowed to have sex while I'm on the phone."

"Then hang up," Cash says. "Because I've got plans and you're interrupting them."

Kase huffs like he's annoyed, but I hear the smile in his voice. "I hate you both."

"You love us," I tell him, nipping and kissing Cash's neck.

"Whatever. I better be the best man."

"Then you better get back here as soon as your concert is over," Cash says, making me freeze and pull back to look at him. He smiles at me, his blue eyes shining. "I'm putting a ring on her finger this week. She's mine now and I'm keeping her."

"What if I want a big wedding?" I whisper, my heart turning somersaults in my chest.

"Little goddess, you can have whatever you want so long as you can get it here this week," he promises me. "We're getting married."

"You didn't ask me to marry you."

"Not gonna ask," he mutters, backing me up against the wall. He pulls my hair free from the red snood I put it in, and then he shimmies my matching dress up my hips. "I told you that you belong to me now. I claimed you when you let me have that tight little cherry. That makes you mine."

"I'm definitely hanging up now," Kase says and then the phone beeps.

"Are you mine then?" I ask Cash, tugging his t-shirt up his body.

"I've been yours, baby." He leans back to let me pull his t-shirt off.

I toss it to the floor, running my hands all over his incredible body. God, he's built like a freaking mountain.

He's got muscles I didn't even know existed in places I didn't even know existed. His tattoos are so damn sexy. He's covered in dark ink and bold geometric patterns. He's gorgeous. And he's all mine.

"I want you in me," I moan, grinding myself down on his hard cock.

"Are you still sore?" he asks, popping the button on his jeans and then tugging the zipper down. His cock springs free, rock hard and begging for attention. The head is an angry red color. The sight of it has me moaning and wiggling all over the place.

"No," I lie. I am still sore, but not badly enough to stop me from having him inside me again. My entire body is aching with need. If he doesn't make love to me soon, I'm going to explode into tiny, frustrated pieces. Thank God we're the only two left in the building.

"Liar." His lips quirk up into a grin before he bites the bottom one and pulls my panties to the side. "That's all right though. I'll take it easy on you this time, little goddess."

"Take it however you want it, Cash. Just get in me," I whine, trying not to lose it when he rubs the head of his cock against my clit, soaking himself in my juices. I'm so ridiculously wet I should probably be embarrassed. I'm not. How can I be when his nostrils flare and his eyes darken with desire?

"Fuck," he groans long and low when he lines up and pushes inside me in one slow thrust. His head drops back, his body trembling against mine. "Goddamn, you feel good, baby."

I writhe against the wall, trying not to cum already. He's so deep like this and it feels so damn good. Like I'm exactly where I'm supposed to be. God, he's so deep. "Please move. I need you."

He fucks me slow, keeping me pinned between his body and the wall like it's easy. He watches my face the entire time, his icy blue eyes roving back and forth like he's trying to memorize the way I look right now. I stare at him too, loving the way his cheeks flush and his eyes dilate until they're a dark, inky blue.

"Dig those heels into my back, Riley," he orders me, yanking the top of my dress down until my boobs spill free. His eyes darken even further at the sight of them. "I want to feel them digging into my skin while you're cumming all over my dick."

Oh, Jesus. I love his filthy mouth.

I do what he says, digging my heels into his back as he picks up the pace, bouncing me up and down on his cock. He dips his head, pulling my nipple into his mouth.

"Cash!" I cry out, my body tightening around him when I feel his teeth in my skin, marking me. I claw his shoulders and then pull his messy hair. Fireworks detonate inside me, sending waves of bliss coursing through my veins.

"Fuck yes," he groans against my boobs, grinding me against him. "Cream all over me, little goddess. Mark me so everyone knows this dick belongs to you."

I writhe, moaning my way through the orgasm. As soon as I go limp, melting into him, he wraps me up in his arms and moves me, plopping me down on my desk. He helps lay me back across the top. All my stuff goes tumbling off the other side again. I don't even care though. Not when he's pulling my legs up toward my chest, spreading me wide for him.

He fucks me hard, rattling my massive desk. I scream and cry out, clinging to the hardwood as he plows into me again and again, fucking me so hard my entire body quakes with each thrust. It feels like he's consuming me completely. I don't ever want him to stop.

And then he starts playing with my clit, jiggling it with one big thumb.

"Cash! Oh fuck. I'm going to...I'm going to–"

"Yeah, you are," he growls, pushing one of my legs straight to change the angle. His eyes are wide and dilated, his expression feral with need. "Cream for me again, little goddess. I want to feel you dripping down my balls before I cum in you."

His filthy words send me over the edge. My entire body convulses, his name ripping from my lips over and over. He roars my name and slams himself into me. He grinds against my clit, prolonging my orgasm as he cums inside me in hot spurts. A combination of our juices drip down the crevice of my ass and onto the top of my desk.

"Goddamn, baby. Goddamn," he whispers, dropping my leg and drooping forward. He nuzzles his face into my chest, pressing sweet little kisses into my skin as we both shake and tremble, coming down. His heart races, pounding like a drum against my stomach.

I thrust a hand into his hair, brushing it back from his face. And then I giggle.

"What's so funny, little goddess?" he asks, groaning as he pushes himself upright to look at me. He's smiling, his expression soft as he looks at me.

"The food is the only thing that didn't fall off the desk," I tell him, still giggling.

His smile widens. He shakes his head and leans down to kiss me before reluctantly pulling out of me. We both groan when he's no longer inside me. I think that's my new favorite place for him. Inside me. He feels so good there.

He reaches into the takeout bag and grabs a few napkins before quickly cleaning between my legs and helping me sit up. Once I'm steady, he tucks himself back inside his pants and then wraps his arms around me, holding me close.

"I love you, little goddess," he whispers into my hair.

My heart turns another somersault as his words work through me, melting me all over again. I might be a bossy, dramatic control freak, but he loves me anyway. I'm not sure how I got so lucky, but I am lucky. "I will marry you, Cash. I want it more than anything."

"Yeah?" he asks, pulling back to look at me.

I nod, my eyes watery. "I love you so much."

He picks me up and sits in my chair, cuddling me up against him. "I've never been happier than I am right now, baby. Thank you for giving me a chance."

"Thank you for chasing me."

"Oh, little goddess. I'm not anywhere close to done chasing you yet," he says, laughing.

Epilogue

CASH

<u>One year later</u>

"Have you seen my wife?" I ask Cami, stopping at her desk.

She glances up from her computer, her green eyes softening when she sees the baby cuddled up on my shoulder asleep.

"Aww, she's so stinking cute," she says, smiling. "That bow is as big as her little head."

"She and her mama like the bows," I say with a shrug. Whatever my girls want, they get. I'm not ashamed to admit I'm wrapped around their little fingers. I fall deeper for my little goddess every day. As soon as I saw the two pink lines on the pregnancy test, I fell for our little one too. Tia is three months old and already looks just like her mama.

She's dramatic like her mama too. She came into the world screaming at the top of her lungs and hasn't stopped yet. The only time she's satisfied is if she's in my arms or her mama's. Luckily, we both work in the same building and can bring her in with us every day.

I tried going back to work after I got my ring on Riley's finger, but I'd only last a few hours before I ended up right back over here. We decided to move me into her building not long later. My office is two doors down from hers. This way, I'm close if she needs me, but I can actually get a little work done without losing my mind worrying about her. It's working out well. Except for the fact that my wife is never in her office. She keeps me chasing after her.

I wouldn't change a single second of it.

"Where's Riley?" I ask again, drawing Cami's attention away from Tia and back to me.

"Um, she should be around here somewhere," Cami says, avoiding my gaze.

I narrow my eyes on her. Like my wife, Cami is a shit liar. They always look everywhere but at me when they're lying. I shake my head at her, chuckling when she buries her face in her hands and groans, knowing she's busted.

"What is she up to this time?" I ask.

"I promised not to tell!"

I briefly consider trying to drag it out of her but decide not to. Riley will kick my ass if I make Cami cry. My woman is sexy as fuck when she's all riled up, but I prefer not to antagonize her when we're working. I can't fuck her to calm her back down when the building is full of people. She's not quiet when I'm in her and those sounds aren't for anyone but me to hear.

"Where's Kase?" I ask instead, patting Tia on the back when she stirs.

"At the studio."

Riley definitely isn't with him then. She's permanently banned from the studio when he's recording. They spend too much time bickering back and forth instead of working. And if she isn't with Kase and she isn't anywhere else I've looked for her, she's left the building.

I'm going to spank her pretty little ass when she gets back. I don't like it when she's out there on her own. She's too damn beautiful and too many men stare at her ass.

That's my ass. It pisses me off when other men look at her like they want her. They can't have her.

"I'll wait in her office," I growl at Cami, stomping toward Riley's office with Tia in my arms.

"Uh oh," Cami whispers behind me.

I let myself into my wife's office and prowl around, looking for a clue where she might have gone. Her office is as neat as ever and her schedule is clear for the afternoon. I mess with the shit on her desk, moving it around. I can't help it. She's so fucking cute when she gets all riled up about me messing with her shit.

Once I'm satisfied that it's suitably fucked up, I stroll toward the couch and lay back with Tia on my chest. She grunts and wiggles her tiny little body. I place a hand on her back and she settles right back down with a sigh.

My heart rolls in my chest. God, I never knew I could love one little human as much as I love this one. She's tiny and perfect, just like her mama. I close my eyes, waiting for Riley to return from wherever the hell she ran off to without telling me.

Less than ten minutes later, I hear her slip inside her office. She's being quiet, like she's trying to keep from waking me, which just makes me smile. After she snuck out of my bed that very first night, I've made a point to know where she's at. Unless she sneaks out of the office—which she doesn't do often because she knows it stresses me out—I can usually find her in under five minutes. It's like she's a magnet, drawing me near. I feel when she's close to me.

"You're in so much trouble, little goddess," I rumble, sitting upright with one hand on Tia's back to keep her secured against me.

"Cash!" Riley jumps and spins in my direction, her hand over her heart. "You scared the crap out of me. I thought you were sleeping."

"And I thought you agreed not to leave the office without telling me," I growl, rising to my feet. I walk toward Tia's bassinet and lay her down, keeping a hand on her back until she settles again. It won't take long before she starts screaming her little head off for her mama and daddy, but I don't need long.

Riley gulps, backing up when I stalk toward her.

"What are you up to this time, little goddess?"

"Nothing," she lies, her back hitting the wall.

"No?" I stop in front of her, so close the fabric of her dress brushes across my arm.

She shakes her head quickly back and forth.

"You look pretty today, baby," I murmur, unable to help myself when my dick turns to steel in my pants. She's in a flirty red dress with a black band around her waist that accentuates her soft curves. The top ties around her neck, pushing those juicy tits up until the soft swells peek from the top. She always looks so fucking pretty in her dresses, exactly like a pin-up model. Her curves are even sexier to me now than they were the first time I laid eyes on her right here in this office.

"Cash," she whispers, the pulse in her throat fluttering.

"Did you lock the door?"

She nods her head, little strands of her hair catching against the wall behind her.

"Good." I smile, dropping to my knees in front of her. "Then you can wrap your thighs around my head and let me eat you."

She whimpers but doesn't stop me when I lift her skirt up and drape one leg over my shoulder. She's already wet, her panties damp with her desire for me. I press a kiss to her inner thigh and then lick across the seam of her panties, groaning at her taste. Somehow, she's even sweeter now.

I tease her through her panties until we're both desperate for it, and then I shove them to the side and attack her pretty little cunt. She cries out, using her hand to muffle the sound as I eat at her. Her taste drives me crazy. It's vanilla and honey and sex and I can't get enough of it.

Her other leg trembles like she's going to fall, so I drape it over my other shoulder, holding her up against the wall as I fuck her with my tongue.

"Cash, oh my God," she moans, digging her hands into my hair and holding on for dear life.

I want to take my time with her, but I know I can't, so I thrust my tongue into her tight little hole and fuck her with it until she's right on the edge. Once she's whimpering my name and begging for relief, I latch onto her clit, sucking hard.

She cries out my name as she explodes apart, soaking me with her juices. I lap them all up, groaning against her cunt. I keep eating her until her body goes limp in my arms and then I press another kiss to her thigh, cover her pussy up again and slide out from beneath her skirts. She's plastered against the wall, her cheeks pink and her lips red where she bit them trying to stay quiet.

"Where were you, baby?" I ask her, nuzzling my face into her neck to plant kisses all over the sensitive skin there.

"I had an appointment."

"What kind of appointment?"

She pushes against my shoulders, not saying anything until I pull back to look at her. Her eyes are narrowed on me and rife with suspicion. "You already know, don't you?"

"Know what?"

"That I'm pregnant!"

I blink at her. "You're pregnant?"

"You didn't know?"

"You're serious, little goddess? You're giving me another baby?"

She bites her lip and nods, her eyes filling with tears. "The doctor just confirmed it. You're going to be a daddy again, Cash."

I pull her into my arms, kissing all over her face as happiness wells in my chest, filling me to overflowing. I'm going to be a daddy again. Holy shit. My little goddess is giving me another baby. Fuck, I hope it's another little girl who looks just like her and Tia.

"Thank you, baby," I whisper, dropping to my knees to kiss her belly. "Thank you. Thank you."

She brushes my hair back from my head, a little sob breaking from her lips. "I love you, Cash."

"I love you too, little goddess." I press my forehead to her belly, blinking back tears. "God, I love you so fucking much, Riley. I never knew I could be this damn happy until I walked into this office and saw you for the first time. Now, every day just gets better and better, baby."

"For me too," she whispers. "You make me so happy, Cash."

"Good, baby." I press another kiss to her belly and then climb to my feet to kiss her hard on the mouth. "Let's get our girl and go home. I need to be inside you."

"Okay," she whispers, staring up at me with dazed eyes filled to the brim with love.

My heart rolls, expanding as I fall a little bit deeper. With her, I'm always falling deeper. I think I always will be. She's not just my missing piece. She's a vital part of me, something so fucking precious and perfect. I don't know what I did to deserve her, but I'm going to spend the rest of my damn life worshipping her like the little goddess she is.

And when I die, I'll worship her in whatever life comes next.

How could I not?

I lead her across the room with one arm wrapped around her to get Tia. Once my baby is tucked against my chest and her diaper back is slung over my shoulder, I lead my woman out of her office. And when we finally make it home and put Tia down, I don't leave the warmth of Riley's body for a long, long time.

It's perfection. Just like she is.

Author's Note

If you enjoyed His Future Bride, please consider leaving a review. Reviews are really important for authors like me.

His Stolen Bride, Kasen and Olivia's story, is now available!

Her Alpha Boss Undercover

"Are you Brooke?"

I spin toward the front door when a deep voice growls my name. The hottest man I've ever seen in my entire life is standing in my doorway. His shoulders are so broad, they almost fill the space. His black hair is unruly, his blue eyes glacial. Like Allison said, he is ripped. His t-shirt stretches across his shoulders, hugging his muscles. His powerful thighs test the seams of his jeans. He looks like he belongs in the mountains, chopping wood and wrestling bears.

His blue eyes are locked on my face and a little growl rumbles in his chest.

"Yes, I'm me. I mean, I'm Brooke."

"Who the fuck is Tim?" he asks, his voice a sharp bark of sound that makes me jump. He sounds angry, but I don't know why.

"Um...the vineyard manager?"

He narrows his eyes on me.

I fight the urge to fidget beneath his stare. It's like he's looking into me, trying to decide if I'm telling him the truth or not. He's intense. Why is that so hot to me?

"You're dating a fellow employee? Isn't there some rule against that?"

"I'm not dating anyone," I huff, feeling defensive and slightly annoyed. Of course he would be hot and a jerk. "And if there is a rule, someone better tell Allison before she sleeps her way through the rest of the staff. Is there a reason you're in my office being a jerk?"

His lips actually twitch like he's going to smile. "You think I'm a jerk?"

"You eavesdropped on a private conversation and then pried into my personal business," I state, tipping my head back to glare at him. "Now, is there a reason you're in my office?"

"My name is Ben Dover. Eli told me I had to come see you."

"Ben Dover?" I eye him skeptically. If his name is Ben Dover, I'm a unicorn. And since I don't have a fancy horn or fly? Well, he's a liar. Eli and Trevor usually have a good sense of people before they hire them, but I think they missed something with this one.

"Go ahead," he drawls, one corner of his lip lifting into a smile. And Jesus. He's even hotter when he's grinning. "Crack your jokes at my expense. But then I get to tease you, Brooke Waters."

I scowl at him, which just makes him chuckle. The rich sound washes over me, sending goosebumps up and down my arms. He's got an incredible laugh.

"I realize my name is rather...unfortunate. You can call me Nate," he says, stepping into my office and holding a hand out toward me. "It's my middle name. I'd appreciate it if you'd keep that first name a secret."

I hesitate for a moment and then slip my hand into his. I jump when electricity races up my arm like he shocked me. His hand dwarfs mine as he wraps it around my entire hand, holding onto me like he's thinking about not letting go.

"Fuck, if you aren't the prettiest little thing I've ever seen," he says, almost like he's talking to himself. His eyes darken as he stares at me, his expression turning absolutely predatory.

A shiver works its way through me, my panties growing damp.

I jerk my hand from his, quickly dropping it to my lap to hide the way it shakes. I can't hide how red my face is though. I can feel my cheeks burning with heat, though I'm not sure if I'm embarrassed or turned on or both.

Both, I think.

"Um...what can I do for you, Nate?" I ask, forcing myself to concentrate.

"You can have dinner with me."

"Sorry, I can't. I have plans."

"With Tim." He's growling again.

"Yes, with Tim." I flick my gaze in his direction to see that he's practically on top of me. And good Lord, he's tall. He towers over me, making me feel small and delicate...two things I have never been in my life. I've always been a bigger girl, and I learned how to stick up for myself a long time ago. Growing up in foster care didn't leave me much of a choice but to stand up for myself because there was no one else willing to do it for me.

"I'll come with you," he says.

"You want to come with me to have dinner with Tim?" I ask, blinking at him.

"Why not? I'm new here. You can show me around, help me get to know the other employees." He smiles at me again, pleading with his eyes for me to agree. They remind me of the way the sky darkens before an afternoon storm rolls in. There are hidden depths to those eyes. And I'm guessing to the man too. "Come on, Brooke Waters. Don't tell me Eli lied about you."

"Lied about me?"

"Mmhmm. He told me hiring you was the best decision he's ever made." A frown crosses his face, making him scowl. "He better not have tried to get between those sexy thighs of yours."

I know he did not just say that to me. My heart flutters over the fact that he thinks any part of me is sexy. My brain is less amused by his crude comment.

"I think you need to leave my office," I snap at him. "Now."

"Not until you agree to have dinner with me, angel baby."

I gape at him, sure he's joking. He's dead serious. I see it in his eyes. "Are you insane?" I splutter. "You just accused me of sleeping with Eli!"

"No, I didn't. I said that horny bastard better not have tried to sleep with you." Nate frowns at me like he's genuinely confused as to why I'm pissed. "I know how Eli is. He can't resist a pretty woman. And angel baby, you are fucking exquisite. It'd be a damn shame if I had to break his jaw for trying to slide between those legs and claim what's mine."

"I think you need your eyes checked," I mutter to him, trying not to melt into a little puddle over the fact that he called me exquisite. "And I'm not yours."

"You will be, Brooke Waters. Just you wait."

Her Alpha Boss Undercover is now available!

Instalove Book Club

The Instalove Book Club is now in session!

Get the inside scoop from your favorite instalove authors, meet new authors to love, and snag freebies and bonus content from featured authors every month. The Instalove Book Club newsletter goes out once per week!

Join now to get your hands on bonus scenes and brand-new, exclusive content from our first six featured authors.

Join the Club: http://instalovebookclub.com

Follow Nichole

Sign-up for the mailing list to stay up to date on all new releases and for exclusive ARC giveaways from Nichole Rose.

Want to connect with Nichole and other readers? Join Nichole Rose's Book Beauties on Facebook!

amazon.com/Nichole-Rose/e/B0847QHXPJ

facebook.com/AuthorNicholeRose/

instagram.com/AuthorNicholeRose

twitter.com/AuthNicholeRose

bookbub.com/authors/nichole-rose

tiktok.com/@authornicholerose

Also Available

<u>Her Alpha Series</u>

Her Alpha Daddy Next Door

Her Alpha Boss Undercover

Her Alpha's Secret Baby

Her Alpha Protector

Her Date with an Alpha

Her Alpha: The Complete Series

<u>Her Bride Series</u>

His Future Bride

His Stolen Bride

His Secret Bride

His Curvy Bride

His Captive Bride

His Blushing Bride

His Bride: The Complete Series

<u>Claimed Series</u>

Possessing Liberty

Teaching Rowan

Claiming Caroline

Kissing Kennedy

Claimed: The Complete Series

<u>Love on the Clock Series</u>

Adore You

Hold You

Keep You

Protect You

Love on the Clock: The Complete Series

<u>The Billionaires' Club</u>

The Billionaire's Big Bold Weakness

The Billionaire's Big Bold Wish

The Billionaire's Big Bold Woman

<u>The Billionaire's Big Bold Wonder</u>

<u>Playing for Keeps</u>

Cutie Pie

Ice Breaker

Ice Prince

Ice Giant (coming soon)

The Second Generation
A Blushing Bride for Christmas

Silver Spoon MC
The Surgeon

The Heir

The Lawyer

The Prodigy (coming soon)

The Bodyguard (coming soon)

Echoes of Forever
His Christmas Miracle

Taken by the Hitman

Wicked Saint

The Ruined Trilogy
Physical Science

Wrecked

Destination Romance
Romancing the Cowboy

Beach House Beauty

<u>Standalone Titles</u>

A Touch of Summer

Black Velvet

Easy Ride

His Secret Obsession

Dirty Boy

Naughty Little Elf

Devil's Deceit

Wearing their Pearls (coming soon)

<u>One Night with You</u>

Falling Hard

Model Behavior

Learning Curve

Angel Kisses

<u>writing with Loni Ree as Loni Nichole</u>

Zane's Rebel (coming soon)

About Nichole Rose

Nichole Rose is a curvy romance author on the west coast. Her books feature headstrong, sassy women and the alpha males who consume them. From grumpy detectives to country boys with attitude to instalove and over-the-top declarations, nothing is off-limits.

Nichole is sure to have a steamy, sweet story just right for everyone. She fully believes the world is ugly enough without trying to fit falling in love into a one-size-fits-all box. When not writing, Nichole enjoys fine wine, cute shoes, and everything supernatural. She is happily married to the love of her life and is a proud mama to the world's most ridiculous fur-babies.

You can learn more about Nichole and her books at her website .

 amazon.com/Nichole-Rose/e/B0847QHXPJ

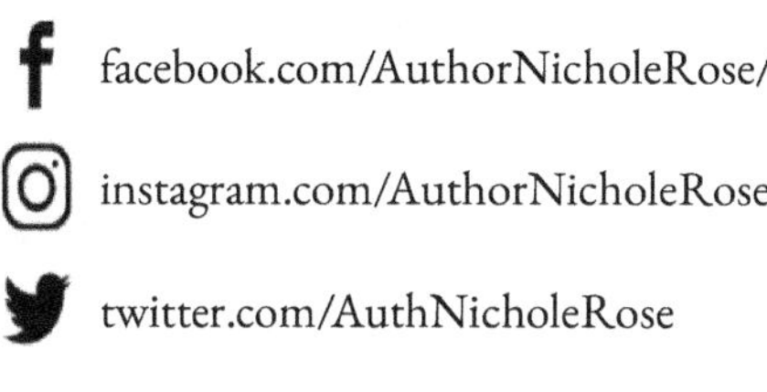

facebook.com/AuthorNicholeRose/

instagram.com/AuthorNicholeRose

twitter.com/AuthNicholeRose

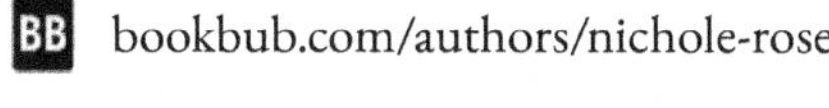

bookbub.com/authors/nichole-rose

tiktok.com/@authornicholerose

www.ingramcontent.com/pod-product-compliance
Lightning Source LLC
Chambersburg PA
CBHW071333130726
47996CB00002B/739